巾幗英雄花木蘭

China's Bravest Girl

The Legend of
Hua Mu Lan

撰述　陳建文 Told by Charlie Chin

插圖　新居富枝 Illustrated by Tomie Arai

翻譯　王性初

Chinese translation by Wang Xing Chu

兒童書籍出版社

Children's Book Press

San Francisco, California

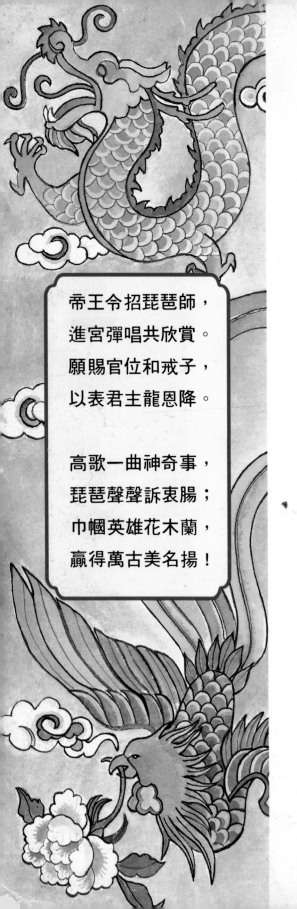

帝王令招琵琶師，
進宮彈唱共欣賞。
願賜官位和戒子，
以表君主龍恩降。

高歌一曲神奇事，
琵琶聲聲訴衷腸；
巾幗英雄花木蘭，
贏得萬古美名揚！

The Emperor called for the Pipa player.
"Have him sing a song of old.
I will give him a seat of honor
and a ring of hammered gold."

The Pipa player took his place
and he sang an ancient story,
the legend of young Hua Mu Lan
the girl who won fame and glory.

2

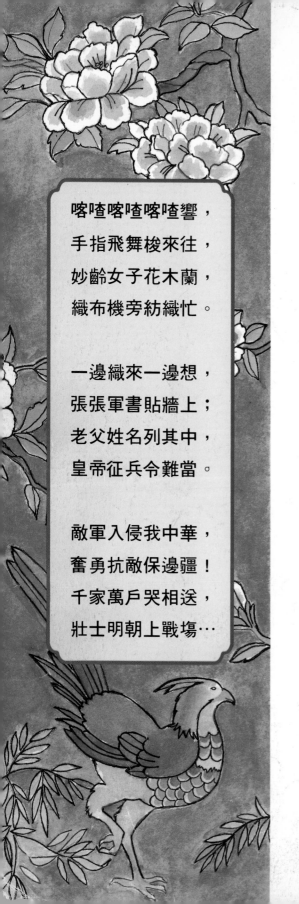

喀喳喀喳喀喳響，
手指飛舞梭來往，
妙齡女子花木蘭，
織布機旁紡織忙。

一邊織來一邊想，
張張軍書貼牆上；
老父姓名列其中，
皇帝征兵令難當。

敵軍入侵我中華，
奮勇抗敵保邊疆！
千家萬戶哭相送，
壯士明朝上戰塲…

The sound is click, and again, click click,
young Hua Mu Lan at the loom.
Her fingers fly, the shuttle darts,
as she weaves inside her room.

Last night she saw the notice.
It was posted on the wall.
On it was her father's name.
He must answer the Emperor's call.

The enemy has invaded China.
Our army must prepare to fight.
One man from every household
must be ready by morning light.

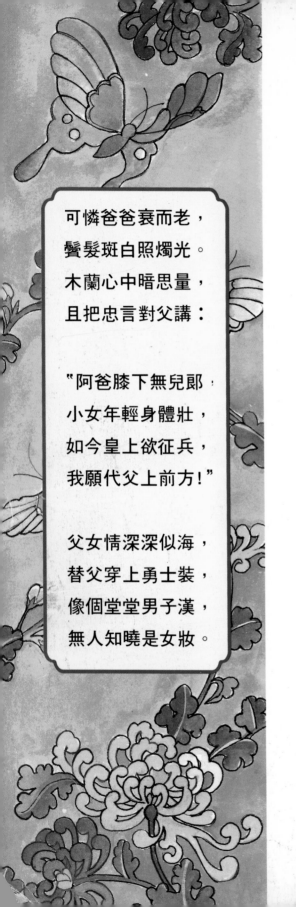

可憐爸爸衰而老，
鬢髮斑白照燭光。
木蘭心中暗思量，
且把忠言對父講：

"阿爸膝下無兒郎，
小女年輕身體壯，
如今皇上欲征兵，
我願代父上前方！"

父女情深深似海，
替父穿上勇士裝，
像個堂堂男子漢，
無人知曉是女妝。

Her father is old and tired.
His hair is turning white.
She tells him of her plan
as they talk by candlelight.

"I am young and healthy,
and you have no eldest son.
If the Emperor needs a soldier,
then I must be the one."

For love of her elderly father
she will dress in warrior's clothes,
walking and talking like a man,
so no one ever knows.

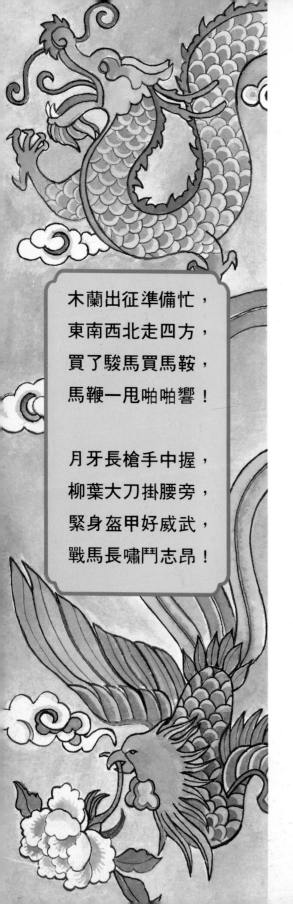

木蘭出征準備忙，
東南西北走四方，
買了駿馬買馬鞍，
馬鞭一甩啪啪響！

月牙長槍手中握，
柳葉大刀掛腰旁，
緊身盔甲好威武，
戰馬長嘯鬥志昂！

She travels in the four directions,
preparing for the trip.
She will buy in different towns
the saddle, horse and whip.

The crescent moon spear in her hand,
the willow leaf sword by her side,
her armor is laced and tightened,
her war horse is saddled to ride.

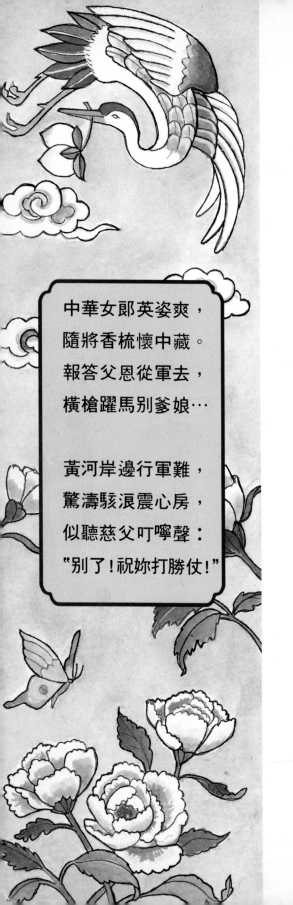

中華女郎英姿爽，
隨將香梳懷中藏。
報答父恩從軍去，
橫槍躍馬別爹娘…

黃河岸邊行軍難，
驚濤駭浪震心房，
似聽慈父叮嚀聲：
"別了！祝妳打勝仗！"

The bravest girl in China
puts away the perfumed comb.
To repay her father's kindness
she will ride away from home.

The banks of the Yellow River
echo the sound of flowing water.
In her heart she hears her father's words,
"Farewell, my faithful daughter."

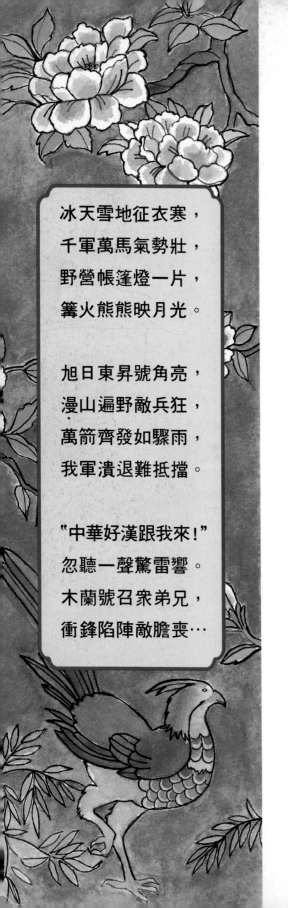

冰天雪地征衣寒，
千軍萬馬氣勢壯，
野營帳篷燈一片，
篝火熊熊映月光。

旭日東昇號角亮，
漫山遍野敵兵狂，
萬箭齊發如驟雨，
我軍潰退難抵擋。

"中華好漢跟我來！"
忽聽一聲驚雷響。
木蘭號召眾弟兄，
衝鋒陷陣敵膽喪…

She joins ten thousand soldiers
camped in the moon-lit snow.
Their tents shine like lanterns
lit by the campfire glow.

The morning light brings the battle.
The invaders take the field.
Enemy arrows find their mark.
China's line begins to yield.

When all seems lost a shout is heard,
"Brave sons of China follow me!"
Warriors wheel and turn about
like the waves of an angry sea.

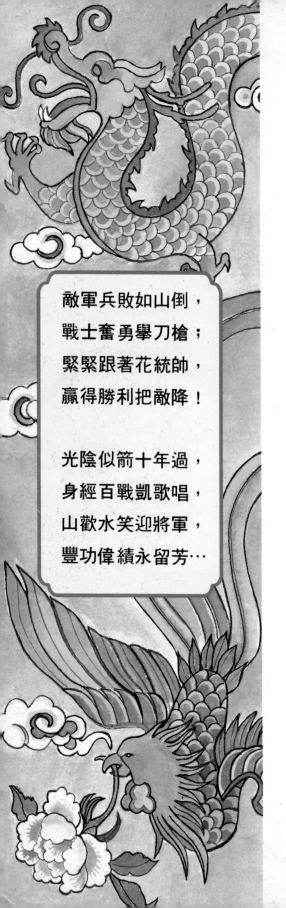

敵軍兵敗如山倒，
戰士奮勇舉刀槍；
緊緊跟著花統帥，
贏得勝利把敵降！

光陰似箭十年過，
身經百戰凱歌唱，
山歡水笑迎將軍，
豐功偉績永留芳…

Cheering troops rally around her.
The enemy line breaks in fear.
Hua Mu Lan's courage wins the day
as she fights with her sword and spear.

She wins in a hundred battles.
Ten years like arrows fly by.
She gains the rank of General.
Her legend will never die.

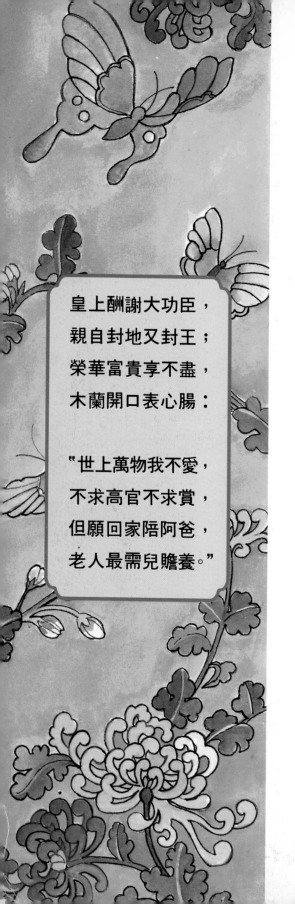

皇上酬謝大功臣，
親自封地又封王；
榮華富貴享不盡，
木蘭開口表心腸：

"世上萬物我不愛，
不求高官不求賞，
但願回家陪阿爸，
老人最需兒贍養。"

The Emperor summons his "hero"
to receive from the royal hand
a minister's post and the title
to a nobleman's house and land.

"There is nothing that I desire,
neither wealth nor minister's post.
My duty is to my father.
In old age, he needs me most."

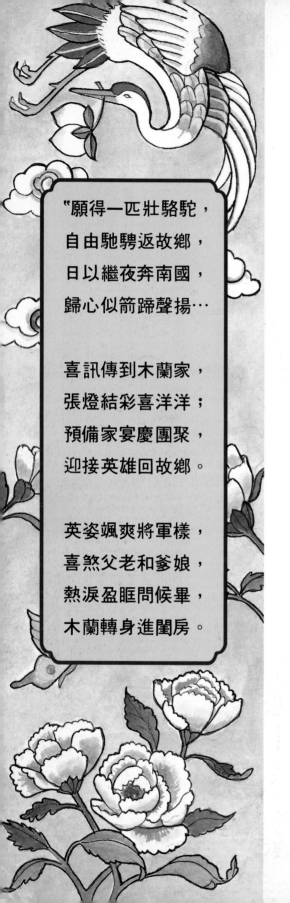

"願得一匹壯駱駝，
自由馳騁返故鄉，
日以繼夜奔南國，
歸心似箭蹄聲揚…

喜訊傳到木蘭家，
張燈結彩喜洋洋；
預備家宴慶團聚，
迎接英雄回故鄉。

英姿颯爽將軍樣，
喜煞父老和爹娘，
熱淚盈眶問候畢，
木蘭轉身進閨房。

"Give me only a strong camel
and my freedom then to roam.
I will ride the southern road
that leads back to my home."

The news is heard at her father's gate
where colorful lanterns burn.
Her family prepares a feast
to celebrate her return.

She enters as a general.
Her father watches with pride.
She greets her father and mother,
then turns to go inside.

20

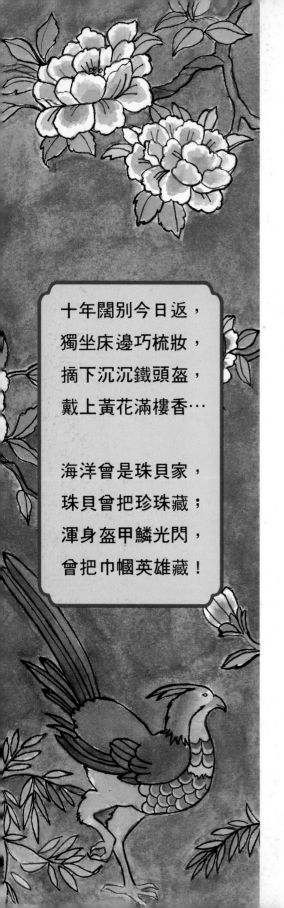

十年闊別今日返，
獨坐床邊巧梳妝，
摘下沉沉鐵頭盔，
戴上黃花滿樓香…

海洋曾是珠貝家，
珠貝曾把珍珠藏；
渾身盔甲鱗光閃，
曾把巾幗英雄藏！

Alone in her room at last,
she sits on her childhood bed.
She takes off the iron helmet
and places flowers on her head.

The ocean hides the oyster.
The oyster hides a pearl.
Bright armor and heavy helmet
hid China's bravest girl.

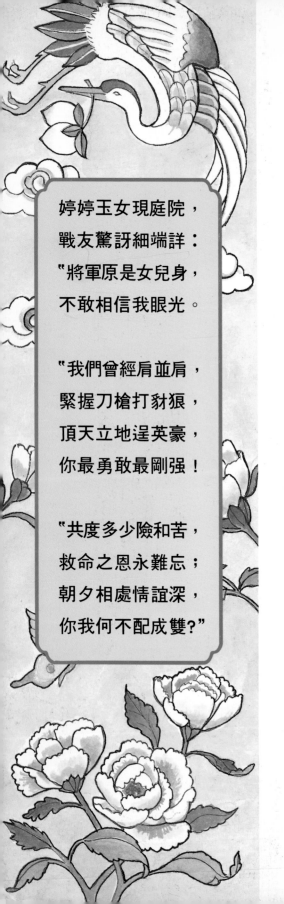

婷婷玉女現庭院，
戰友驚訝細端詳：
"將軍原是女兒身，
不敢相信我眼光。

"我們曾經肩並肩，
緊握刀槍打豺狼，
頂天立地逞英豪，
你最勇敢最剛強！

"共度多少險和苦，
救命之恩永難忘；
朝夕相處情誼深，
你我何不配成雙?"

As she steps into the courtyard,
her comrade says in surprise,
"My general has become a woman.
I can't believe my eyes!

"We fought shoulder to shoulder.
Our hands gripped sword and spear.
I knew you as a warrior
who was strong and without fear.

"How many times in danger
did you turn to save my life?
We were always the best of friends.
Why not become husband and wife?"

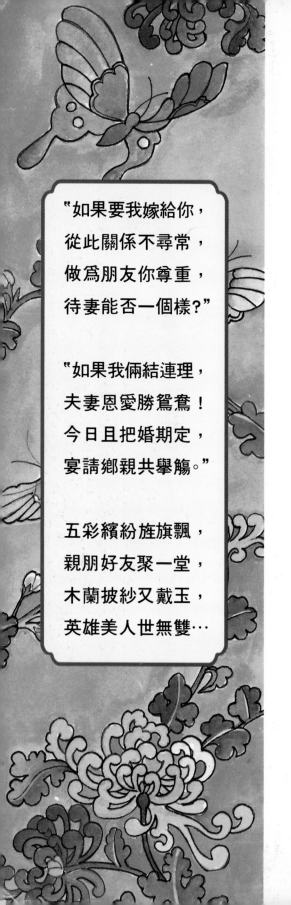

"如果要我嫁給你，
從此關係不尋常，
做爲朋友你尊重，
待妻能否一個樣?"

"如果我倆結連理，
夫妻恩愛勝鴛鴦!
今日且把婚期定，
宴請鄉親共舉觴。"

五彩繽紛旌旗飄，
親朋好友聚一堂，
木蘭披紗又戴玉，
英雄美人世無雙…

"If I become your wife," she says,
"we will play a different game.
You treat your friends with honor.
Can your wife expect the same?"

"Yes, I will honor you," he says,
"in all I do and say.
Now let's invite the villagers
and set the wedding day."

Red and gold banners adorn the house.
A banquet is prepared for all.
She wears the finest jade and silk
for the wedding in her husband's hall.

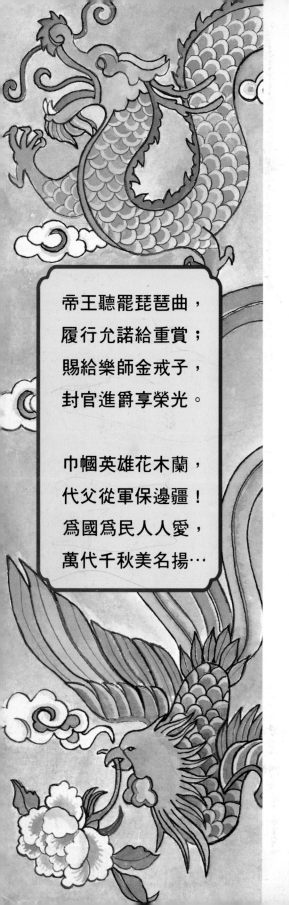

帝王聽罷琵琶曲，
履行允諾給重賞；
賜給樂師金戒子，
封官進爵享榮光。

巾幗英雄花木蘭，
代父從軍保邊疆！
爲國爲民人人愛，
萬代千秋美名揚…

The Pipa player sang the last verse
His rewards had been foretold:
for his skill a seat of honor;
for his song a ring of gold.

The legend of young Hua Mu Lan
whose bravery saved her nation
is loved by the Chinese people
and retold each generation.

The Legend of Hua Mu Lan is based on a poem called "Mu Lan Ci,"
which was recorded in the Soong Dynasty (AD 960-1279).

Charlie Chin is a writer, musician, composer and actor. For many years he was the Education Director of the Chinatown History Museum in New York City. He has always been fascinated with the story of Hua Mu Lan and how her legend has changed and yet survived over the centuries. He lives in the San Francisco Bay Area with his wife and son.

Tomie Arai has spent most of the last 16 years working in New York neighborhoods as a muralist and community artist. Her work has appeared in numerous Asian-American women's anthologies and is in the collection of the Museum of Modern Art in New York City. She lives in New York City with her husband and two children. She is the illustrator of *Sachiko Means Happiness*, also published by Children's Book Press.

Translator **Wang Xing Chu** is a poet, author, critic, and a specialist in classical Chinese literature. His works have appeared in China, Hong Kong, Thailand and Taiwan. A native of China, he and his wife currently live in San Francisco, California.

Story copyright (c) 1993 by Charlie Chin. All rights reserved.
Illustrations copyright (c) 1993 by Tomie Arai. All rights reserved.
Chinese translation copyright (c) 1993 by Children's Book Press. All rights reserved.
Editors: Harriet Rohmer and David Schecter   Design: Nancy Hom   Production: Tony Yuen
Photography: Lee Fatherree   Title English lettering: Lily Lee   Chinese typesetting: Katherine Loh

Thanks to Eva Chow, Nancy Hom, Maywan Shen Krach, Gimmy Park Li, Suzanne Low, Norine Nishimura, Jeff Wang, Wang Xing Chu , Patty Wong, Siu Mui Wu, Tony Yuen, and Judy Yung for their help and advice.

Children's Book Press is a nonprofit community publisher. Publication of this book has been supported in part by grants from the California Arts Council, the Wallace Alexander Gerbode Foundation, the Fleishhacker Foundation, the Neutrogena Corporation, the Morris Stulsaft Foundation, the Louis R. Lurie Foundation, the Prudential Foundation, and others, as part of our "Books About You and Me" outreach project.

Library of Congress Cataloging-in-Publication Data
Chin, Charlie.
   China's bravest girl: the legend of Hua Mu Lan = [Chin kuo ying hsiung Hua Mu-lan] / told by Charlie Chin; illustrated by Tomie Arai; Chinese translation by Wang Xing Chu.   p. cm.
   English and Chinese. Parallel title in Chinese characters.
   Summary: Legend of Hua Mu Lan who goes to war disguised as a man to save the family honor and becomes a great general.
   ISBN 0-89239-120-0
   1. Hua, Mu-lan (Legendary character)–Juvenile poetry. I. Arai, Tomie, ill.   II. Wang, Xing Chu.   III. Title.
IV. Title: Legend of Hua Mu Lan.   V. Title: Chin kuo ying hsiung Hua Mu-lan.
PS3553.H4896C48   1993   398.21—dc20   93-15255   CIP

Printed in China through Marwin Productions
10 9 8 7 6 5 4 3 2 1